Runaway

ANNELLE HAMMAN

Literary Freedom Publishing, LLC
Visit our website:
www.literaryfreedompub.com

Runaway

Cover Design by Writluxe University.

Annelle Hamman asserts the moral right to be identified as the author of this work.

Printed in the United States of America.

First Printing: September 2024

Literary Freedom Publishing, LLC.

Contents

Jack Scott

❦

I smile in the mirror while fixing my tie. "God, I suck at this." I suck my teeth then glance at my brother as he walks over. We study each other for a moment, then I blurt, "How did you learn how to tie ties?"

A faint smile grows on his face. "I learned from Dad! Remember he used to work at that funeral parlor?"

My ears redden as I consider the fact that I forgot about that. Jacob used to go with Dad every now and then to help.

I clear my throat to regather my bearings. "Yes, I forgot about that."

Jacob chuckles, not seeming to notice I'm masking my embarrassment about not remembering where our father worked. "Well, it has been four years..." His smile fades a little. We don't talk about Dad a lot. Not since his death.

When dad died, I felt like our family became duller and depressing.

Dad didn't die in a big way, like getting murdered or doing something dumb, but he did die of a heart condition. He always said it didn't hurt much but I know it hurt enough for him to take pain medication.

I pull Jacob into a tight hug. "Love you, bro; thanks for coming here to be my best man."

Jacob doesn't say anything, but he smiles and hugs me back.

Once we finish the hug, my brother leans down and fixes my tie. "I hope you have a lovely wedding day, lil bro." He's always called me that, though he's only two years older than me.

It suddenly dawns on me to question him. "Why don't you ever call me by my name?" Jacob laughs. I love and hate his laugh. It's contagious, and we both burst out in laughter. "You're right, Jack, you're a grown man now. I can call you by your name."

We continue our laughter til it naturally subsides.

Camie James

I'm pacing across my dressing room and Veronika is sitting on one of those couch-like seats watching me.

"I can't! I just can't…" I'm screaming at my best friend.

She stares at me in bewilderment, likely wondering where my outburst is coming from. "Camie, you don't have to marry him if you don't want to. It's okay!"

I relax now that I realize she's on my side no matter what. "I don't want to marry him," I admit, "but if I don't, my family will track me down, including Jack!" I plop down into my seat because if I keep pacing the room I might faint. Dizziness consumes me and I can feel this dumb wedding dress under my butt, rubbing against the back of my leg. It's so itchy. I wanted a shorter dress because it reminded me of a pirate. I love pirates, but it reminded my mom of the same thing. My mom hates pirates, especially the female ones because she thinks they're un-lady-like. So I got stuck with this heavy, itchy long dress, then she had the audacity to not come to the wedding.

I hate her sometimes… actually, all the time. Then I realize, "Dang it! I forgot my medicine!"

Veronika turns to me. "There's no way you did. I could've sworn I packed it in your bag for you?" She drops to the floor to check my bag. I'm right - no medicine. She freaks out a bit, then stops and grabs her bag. She pulls something out.

"My medicine!" I gush. "Thank you!" I need to take this medicine twice a day because of my anxiety. It doesn't do that much but it helps a bit. I grab a water bottle and swallow one pill.

Jack Scott

I finish getting ready just in time for me to go out. I play with my collar a bit, then my hair. Jacob had to leave a few minutes ago to help Calob, our younger brother.

I look over, grab my wallet, and open it, staring at the picture inside. It's Dad. I tear up a little, then wipe the tears away as soon as I hear someone open the door.

"Jacob?"

Mom's head pops out behind the door. "Nope, just your old lady mother!"

I laugh because she isn't that old. She's only nineteen years older than me. I'm twenty-four. "Mom, you're not that old. Just wait another twenty years, then you can say that."

We both laugh. I love my mother's laugh; she's so beautiful. "I'm glad you could make it. It means a lot to me."

She stops laughing and smiles, pulls my head

down, and kisses my forehead. "Of course, sweetheart; what kind of mother would miss her child's wedding?" She looks at me for a moment, then hugs me. She leans out and examines my hair. "Ew!" She licks her hand and rubs it against my head.

"Mooommm! My hair looks fine!"

She rolls her eyes, grabs a comb and some hair gel, and starts messing with my hair even more. Five minutes later, she's done. "It looks so good."

Camie James

I grab a pair of scissors and start cutting up my wedding dress. Veronika works on the rest of it, but this stupid dress is so thick we're barely able to cut through it. Once we finally finish, I grab her hand and we run to the bathroom. I climb on the toilet and push the window open. It takes ten minutes to do. Once it finally opens, we jump through it. We're on the first floor so it's safe. We take off running again.

Once we find the parking lot, we sprint to her sister's car. Veronika's sister is the only person with a license who's stupid enough to leave her keys in the car. We would've taken our cars but Veronika isn't legally allowed to drive and my mother made sure I was driven here by someone else.

We get in and I grab her keys, start the car and we drive away. After a few seconds, I slam on the breaks and check to make sure I have all my stuff.

"My phone, your phone, cash, driver's licenses, makeup, a picture of my siblings, Daniel's phone number, and… wait! I still have Daniel's phone number!" Veronika remembers Daniel as 'cute boy'. We met him while we were at this nice restaurant. I spilled food all over the ground and he helped me clean it up. Veronika's eyes widen. "You should call him. Tell him to meet us at that bar!" I get excited and pull my phone and the paper closer to me to make sure I don't get the number wrong.

Jack Scott

❧

I t's finally time. I'm standing here and all I must do now is wait for my lovely wife. She'd better be lovely at least, or we're going to have problems.

I look over at my brothers, then the bridesmaids. 'That's weird that my wife's best friend isn't here. She was with her in the dressing room...'

I smile as I wait three minutes, then eight more minutes. I send two bridesmaids to look for her. Thirteen minutes later, I ask my mother if she can look in the bathrooms. Twenty-six minutes later...

"Holy smokes!" Camie's best friend's sister walks into the room yelling. "I think she stole my car!"

My brother taps my shoulder. I turned around.

"Hey, Calob needs to go to bed. It's past

eight o'clock. I don't think she's coming, sorry dude."

He walks away with Calob.

Those words sting. They sound like something... I would say to... hurt someone. Realization dawns. She isn't coming. Not just because she doesn't love me but because of how I act. How I treat her. My stupid attitude drove her away. That has to be the reason.

I'll fix my attitude and tone, then once I'm perfect I'll find her and she'll become my wife!

Camie James

❦

"Did we just do that?" I chuckle and so does she.

"Yes, we did!" We burst into a fit of giggles.

After a few moments, I wipe my happy tears, probably smearing my mascara along the way. "I'm so happy I don't have to be with him."

We drive up to a gas station so we can fill the car up.

I turn to Veronika. "I'll be right back. I'm going to pay for the gas."

"'Kay." She nods.

I go in and ask the lady for twenty dollars on pump twelve. I walk back out and fill the tank, then hop back in.

"Actually, you want some snacks? I stole his wallet!" Veronika said.

I burst out into a new bout of laughter. "Omg, you didn't!" I grab the wallet and she was right; this is his wallet. I take twenty bucks and we go inside to get food. Afterward, we re-enter the car and drive away.

We go to the club to see Daniel, the cute guy I met. I had texted him earlier to tell him where we would be and hoped he would show up. We walk in and find him a lot quicker than we thought we would. After a few minutes, Veronica and Daniel get some drinks. I'm driving after this so I only have one drink.

Some time later, Daniel starts acting weird.

"I think I'm, um… going to go to the bathroom," he says. As he gets up, he almost falls but catches himself.

Now it's been ten minutes and I'm guessing he's not coming back. I shrug as I grab Veronika and we start heading out the door.

I get Veronika through the door and hop into the driver's seat. I grab my seat belt and then I see Daniel on the ground lying there like a weird drunk. I drive off.

We can hear the wind gliding across our ears, smiles on our faces as we exit the parking lot to the road and then to another state.

Jack Scott

I'm sitting on my couch in the family house. I grab the remote to turn down the volume from twenty to fifteen and lean my head back. I have no clue what good deed I should do to win Carmie back.

"Ugh! Brother, come here!" I turn off the television.

My brother comes into the room quietly. He doesn't look happy. "Can you kindly shut up? Calob is trying to sleep!" he whisper-screams at me.

"I don't care!" I say as I roll my eyes. Wait... this could be a good deed! "I apologize," I whisper.

My brother's eyes widen. "Oh?" He looks like he is questioning me. "Really, you're sorry?" He laughs but quickly stops himself so he doesn't wake up our brother. "That is the funniest joke you've ever told!" He quietly tries to stop laughing.

"I'm not joking." I have to keep calm because if I don't, I won't be doing a good deed. I roll my eyes because my brother is so stupid.

"Really?" he says, now calm. "Wow, her leaving you really did hurt you. Didn't know it would make you think about anyone but yourself, for once."

It takes me a moment to hear what he said under his breath but when I do, I say, "Okay but... excuse me?" I clap my hands over my mouth and gasp, realizing I spoke too loud.

"Great, you woke up Calob." He stomps away to put him back to sleep.

Maybe I do need help with my temper...

Camie James

Around two hours ago, when Veronika sobered up, we switched seats so I could take an hour nap.

We arrive at a motel. It's small but also cute.

"Come on!" Veronika says.

I'm confused. We didn't call any motels about a reservation.

"By the way, don't worry. I called them while we were at the gas station." She smiles at me.

"Oh thanks, I was kind of confused." I laugh softly.

We walk inside and retrieve our keys to the room. "Alright, you gals are in room 408. Also, we don't serve dinner, sorry."

"It's okay, we have food," I say to the kind old man. He gives us a friendly smile as we leave the lobby.

We get to the door of our room. "Let's go!"

Veronika yells, grabbing her key and opening the door.

When we get inside, it's beautiful. We have a huge window that has a wonderful view. My worries disappear. "I think this might just be your best idea ever, Veronika."

She rolls her eyes. "Duh!" She can't help but laugh at herself. "I knew that you were better off without him. You deserve so much better than him."

I look around and let out a small sigh of relief. "I'm glad we did this."

I smile.

Jack Scott

I stand in front of my bed. "She really did leave me," I think. "Of course she did, you idiot, why did you think she'd come back? She abandoned you at your wedding! Why would she come back to you after that?"

I hold back the tears that are fighting to pour out of my eyes. It hurts. I take off my shirt and tie and sit on my bed. I think about all that happened and how I could've made her want to stay. Was it my constant yelling? Maybe my drinking or smoking? Maybe it was me working constantly and not giving her enough attention?

What if I gave her flowers? Would she have stayed? I don't know, what if it was just me? What if I just wasn't enough for her? Maybe I'm ugly? Do I need plastic surgery or Botox? Maybe just working out?

I spend hours thinking of ways I could have made her stay, or how I can convince her to come back. But what if we just aren't meant to be together? Her mom said we were perfect for each other. Why would a mother lie? I slam my face into my pillow and cry my eyes out after hours of holding my tears in.

I cry myself to sleep.

Camie James
༄

I had a wonderful night's sleep. I'm well rested and I feel great. Veronika is already awake and dressed. "Is that breakfast?" I ask.

She laughs and holds up the McDonald's bag. "What else would this be, dinner? It's only 8:20."

I look at the time on my phone and she's right. As I'm about to put down my phone, I notice a notification. *Mom,* I read. "Oh, God! I forgot to block her."

I open my phone and read the message.

> I cannot believe you didn't show up last night. You should be ashamed! He looked so lonely, so sad! Do you really want to be the cause of someone's misery?

Of course, she's trying to make me feel bad

so I'll apologize then get married to that toxic boy. I begin typing,

> Well, you could've at least come to say something to me before you didn't even show up. How do you know I didn't get married?

Veronika walks over and reads over my shoulder "God, I always hated her, such a bad influence on you!" she says in a goofy voice.

I laugh a little, then hug her. "Alright, give me my breakfast! I'm starving!" I say long and dramatically. It makes both of us laugh and she grabs the sandwiches out of the bag and hands me one. I hope we stay friends forever.

Ha, I sound like a little kid.

Jack Scott

I wake up. It's bright outside. I turn over and notice the bed is empty apart from me. Right, I didn't get married. I feel like yelling. How could I be so stupid? I sigh. "Okay, I should get ready for the day. I have a week off work and I'm going to use it."

But the question is, what will I use my extra time for? "Oh, that makes sense. To become a better and nicer person for her! Ugh, why did Camie leave me?"

After agonizing a few more moments I conclude that I'm a useless husband and I can't do anything right.

I take a deep breath, get dressed, brush my teeth, hair and get ready to go and see my brothers. As I leave, I stop and look in the mirror. "I need to shave. Camie always said she didn't like my beard…"

Camie James

I stare in the mirror, smoothing out my new blouse. "Is this an okay outfit?"

"Hm…" Veronika looks me over. "Is that from my closet?" She lets out a small laugh.

"It might be? Sorry I just grabbed the first outfit I saw, and thought it looked good." I forgot we were sharing a closet now. I'm used to having my own closet to myself. I start to take off the shirt, but Veronika stops me.

"Girl, you can wear it; it's okay." She gives me a bright smile.

I smile back, fix my shirt, and grab my bag and keys. "I'm going to go to the store; need anything?"

Veronika thinks for a second. "Hm, uh yeah!"

I wait for her to continue, but she jumps up and puts on some shoes. She's in her pajamas; what's she doing?

"I'm coming with you!"

"Um, okay." I shoot her a weird look.

"Let's go."

Once we get to the store, we grab a cart and start shopping. We get normal groceries, vegetables, fruits, meats, desserts, and some candy just for fun!

When we head to the cash register, Veronika has to go get something. She doesn't tell me what it is though. I unpack my cart and the cashier starts to scan items, but he stops in the middle of it.

"Hey, you're pretty cute."

I look up from my wallet. "Thank you."

I smile at him. He looks like he's around seventeen. I don't want to hurt the kid's feelings. "You're a cute kid." I stop myself from talking. I didn't mean to say that out loud. I must have spaced out a little. Veronika is back with bread.

He finishes scanning, and we pay and leave. I think I hurt his feelings.

Jack Scott

I wash the beard hair out of my razor, then look up at the mirror as I grab a Band-Aid.

"Ow, how'd I mess up this bad?"

I use a cotton ball to wipe off some of the blood. I guess it's karma, or because I haven't shaved in four years. I apply the Band-Aid to the cut.

"Jeez, couldn't I just have paid someone to do it for me?" I grab a random gray shirt and some jeans. "It's kind of cold. I should grab a jacket too."

As I say that, I look at my feet. "Right stupid, you need shoes to go outside."

I put on some shoes, and a jacket and walk out the door. When I get to my brother's, I knock on the door and as it opens he sees the bandages on my face.

"Jesus Christ!"

I roll my eyes.

"Sorry," he says, "but what happened?"

I look down, trying not to make it obvious that I'm feeling embarrassed. "I tried to shave my beard."

"Shave your beard or cut your face off?" He bursts out laughing, as I sigh and I rolled my eyes. I seem to be doing that a lot these days.

"I'm sorry, but did you really think you would just know how to shave?" He was clearly holding in a laugh.

"You can laugh if you want," I reassure him. "I understand, it's funny. I should have come to you for help."

He looks at me for a moment. "Do you want to come in?"

I smile as I walk in.

Camie James

‿❧‿

As me and Veronika walk inside our room,
I put down the bags I'm holding and
jump on the bed. For a motel, these
beds are comfortable.

"I know you aren't about to make me put all of
these groceries away by myself?" Veronika puts
the bags on the counter. I can tell she's trying not
to laugh.

I smile as I get up off the bed and throw my
shoes in the closet. I grab the bags on the floor
and help her put the groceries away. After that,
we sit and watch a children's movie.

. . .

When the movie ends we don't realize it because we got bored and started to play on our phones.

I'm playing Candy Crush when I hear a weird noise from in front of me, I look up; it's just the television.

I laugh and lay my head back, cover myself with a blanket, and go back to sleep.

Jack Scott

I step into Jacob's house and take my shoes off. I sit on the couch as we hear a little voice say my name.

"Hey Calob, what are you doing?"

"I just woke up from my nap." He stares down at the floor, holding a stuffed bear.

I tap a seat on the couch as a way to tell him to come sit with me.

He jumps with excitement and runs over. As he sits down, he grabs my arm and lays his head down.

Jacob laughs as he turns to me. "Anyway, what did you need to talk about?"

He has a bright smile on his face. It's so sweet; I wish I had such a smile. I love how each time he smiles, everyone notices. I'm lucky to have an amazing brother. If only I was as awesome as him...

"Hey! You okay?" Jacob asks with concern.

I snap out of it. "I'm okay."

Jacob stares at me expectantly. He knows I came here for a reason, so I should just let it out. So I do.

"Okay, the reason I came here was because I wanted to ask you for some... Um, well..." I look over at Calob and sigh. "I need some advice, please."

Jacob smiles. "Of course, I will help you; you're my brother. I love you."

Those words feel weird to hear. I don't feel used to hearing such positive things, even though my family is so happy all the time. It feels weird to think that somebody is willing to help me.

Camie James

I'm sitting in a coffee shop with Veronika. I've been doing so much since I last saw Jack. Me and Veronika haven't been able to really talk that much since she moved to Canada.

I still don't really understand why she wanted to move to Canada, but I'm not going to ask why.

"Ma'am, here's your coffee."

I put my phone down. "Thank you, sweetie." I smile at her as she walks away.

"How have you been the last five years?" Veronika asks me as I take a sip of my coffee.

"I'm doing amazing; I got a really good job!"

Veronika's outfit is so pretty and it looks like she lost some weight. "That's awesome. I've been doing great too. I lost twenty pounds."

I can tell she couldn't wait to tell me that.

"That's awesome, I'm so proud of you!" I really am proud of her.

After a while of talking, we get up to walk around the mall. As we're leaving the coffee shop, I throw away my cup.

We walk around and talk about what we've done and how things have been since we've last seen each other. I'm distracted for a moment, so I don't realize someone is walking toward me until I accidentally run into them.

"Camie?"

"Jack?" I reach my hand out to help him up, "How are you? It's been so long since I've last seen you."

Veronika rolls her eyes.

He grabs my hand and stands to his feet. His clothes look raggedy and dirty. *I wonder how long it's been since he's showered?*

"I'm okay. Sorry about how I look right now."

I laugh a little; he does look messy.

"It's fine." I smile.

"I promise, I own better clothes than this! I'm actually buying clothes right now," he says.

"Okay, well hope you have fun, are you doing okay though? Since I, well, kind of ran away from our wedding?"

He looks over and so do I. *It's his brother Jacob; he's grown a lot. Calob. He looks like he is in tenth grade now. Wow, he's grown a lot too.*

"Hey Camie, we should probably go now. I

still want to hang out with my friend, you know.
We still have lots of catching up to do," Veronica
says, giving Jack a dirty look.

I can see she still hates Jack.

"Right, bye Jack. I hope you do well." I
walk off.

I think this might be our last interaction.

Jack Scott

I've been a little sad after Camie left me, but in the last two years, I've been feeling a lot more joyful since I realized she will never really love me. I've accepted it and I like to imagine she's having an amazing life. I actually got fired from my original job but I got a new one. It pays less but I can still afford my house so I'm okay with it.

I decided to go to this store for some nice clothes. I finally have a nice job and I think I've finally gotten over Camie. I mean it only took me five years.

I decided to bring my brothers with me. Calob just finished ninth grade and is about to start tenth. Jacob has worn out most of his clothes since he started working out.

I start to head to Old Navy 'cause the clothes are in the budget I set for myself, plus Calob likes the clothes from there.

To be honest I think almost his entire closet is Old Navy clothes… that's funny.

As we start heading that way, I ask Calob to go buy me and him a frozen yogurt and to meet me and Jacob at the store.

Jacob and I begin to plan a trip to Mexico. Not sure how this conversation started but he looks excited that we're making plans. I mention some cool waterfalls nearby and that we should buy some swimsuits, but I accidentally make Jacob need to go pee with the mention of water.

I keep walking as he heads to the bathroom, but someone runs into me. I end up tripping on my butt, but when I look at who it is.

"Camie?" I say.

"Jack?" She gives me her hand, "How are you? It's been so long since I've last seen you." I see Veronika behind her. She's not thrilled to see me.

I grab her hand and stand to my feet. She looks like she's doing great.

"It's fine." I smile. "I promise, I own better clothes than this! I'm actually buying clothes right now."

.   .   .

"Okay, well hope you have fun, are you doing okay though? Since I, well kind of ran away from our wedding?"

I hear a faint noise, so I look over. *It's Jacob, and Calob's coming with our frozen yogurt.*

I go back to looking at Camie.

"Hey Camie, we should probably go now. I still want to hang out with my friend, you know. We still have lots of catching up to do," Veronica says.

I know Veronika still hates me. Well, I guess she does have some good reasons. I didn't treat her best friend well when we were together.

I wave goodbye to Camie and Veronika as I put my hand on Calob's back and I grab my frozen yogurt from him. I'm glad that they're doing well. I hug Calob.

I think this might be our last interaction.

Made in the USA
Monee, IL
30 September 2024

66845511R00024